Muffkins on Parade

By V. Gilbert Beers

Illustrated by Helen Endres

MOODY PRESS • CHICAGO

What You Will Find in This Book

© 1982 by V. Gilbert Beers

Library of Congress Cataloging in Publication Data

Beers, V. Gilbert (Victor Gilbert), 1928-
   Muffkins on parade.

   SUMMARY: A collection of Bible stories coupled with related adventures of the Muffin family, each accompanied by summaries and questions.

   1. Bible stories, English. (1. Bible stories. 2 Christian life-Fiction) I. Title.

BS551.2.B4385   220.9'505   82-6338
ISBN 0-8024-9572-9   AACR2
2 3 4 5 6 7 Printing WP Year 88 87 86 85 84
Printed in the United States of America

TO PARENTS AND TEACHERS

MUFFKINS ON PARADE is a Bible story book, with stories of famous Bible people. But this book presents Bible stories in a new, exciting way. Each Bible story is coupled with a Muffin Family adventure that shows Bible truth at work in a family like yours and mine. That Bible truth is summarized at the close of each Bible story, along with questions to help your child understand it. The matching Muffin Family story applies the same Bible truth. The application is clearly stated at the end of each Muffin story, accompanied by questions to help your child put that truth to work in his or her own life. Some application stories are about the Muffin Family characters—Mommi, Poppi, Maxi, Mini, and their pets, Ruff and Tuff. Other application stories are about the Muffkins, make-believe characters that add fun and fantasy. This book is one volume of a series called THE MUFFIN FAMILY PICTURE BIBLE, in which Bible and modern life, truth and fantasy, and you and the Muffins all meet at a certain place. Here you meet in the midst of a Muffkin parade. Other volumes in this series are: THROUGH GOLDEN WINDOWS, UNDER THE TAGALONG TREE, WITH SAILS TO THE WIND, OVER BUTTONWOOD BRIDGE, FROM CASTLES IN THE CLOUDS, WITH MAXI AND MINI IN MUFFKINLAND, OUT OF THE TREASURE CHEST, ALONG THIMBLELANE TRAILS, and TREEHOUSE TALES.

FOLLOW ME!

Who Knows the Way?

John 1:35-51

"Do you see Jesus over there?" John the Baptist asked two of his friends. "He is the Lamb of God!"

The two friends stared at Jesus. "The Lamb of God?" they must have whispered. "Does he mean that Jesus is God's Son?"

That was exactly what John meant. Jesus was not just an ordinary man. He was God's Son! If anyone wanted to know about God and His home, who could tell them more than Jesus? If anyone wanted to know how to go to God, who could help them more than Jesus?

"Let's go," said one of the friends. So the two of them hurried off after Jesus. They wanted to follow Him and learn what He had to say.

"What do you want?" Jesus asked when He saw them coming.

"We want to see Your home," they answered.

"Come with Me," said Jesus. They went with Jesus to the place where He was staying. That afternoon they stayed with Jesus until four o'clock, listening to Him.

Andrew, one of those two men, went to find his brother, Simon. He was excited. He was sure now that Jesus was God's Son, and he wanted Simon to meet Him, too.

"We have found Him!" Andrew shouted when he found Simon.

"Found who?" asked Simon.

"God's Son!" said Andrew. "Come with me and meet Him!"

Simon hurried off with his brother Andrew. Before long, he stood before Jesus.

Simon stared at Jesus. Was Andrew right? Was this truly God's Son?

Jesus looked into Simon's eyes. "Since you will follow Me, I will give you a new name," He said. "You have been known as Simon, John's son. But now I will name you Peter." Peter's new name meant "a rock."

The next day Jesus headed toward Galilee. Along the way he met Philip, from the town of Bethsaida in Galilee.

"Come with Me and be My follower," Jesus said. Someone must have told Philip about Jesus, because he was ready to follow Him. He knew that Jesus was God's Son and could tell him much about God and heaven.

Philip was so excited about following Jesus that he ran to find his friend Nathanael. "We have found God's Son!" he shouted when he saw his friend. "His name is Jesus. He is the son of Joseph of Nazareth."

"Nazareth?" said Nathanael. "That town? How could God's Son come from THERE?"

"Come and meet Him!" said Philip. "See for yourself!"

Nathanael went with Philip. He must have grumbled a little as he went. God's Son? From Nazareth? How could this be?

"Look!" Jesus said as Nathanael came toward him. "Here comes a truly good man."

"How do you know?" asked Nathanael.

"I know all about you," said Jesus. "I saw you sitting under that fig tree before Philip found you."

Nathanael stared at Jesus. How could that be? No man could do that! Then Nathanael knew. This was not an ordinary man. Jesus must really be God's Son.

"You ARE God's Son, the King of Israel!" Nathanael whispered.

"That was such a little thing that caused you to believe in Me," said Jesus. "But you will see much greater things than this. You will some day see heaven open. And you will see God's angels going back and forth between heaven and earth."

Jesus headed back toward Galilee. He was not alone now. Four men followed Him—Peter, Andrew, Philip, and Nathanael. Each man knew that Jesus was more than just a man. He was God's Son. They would go where He went. They would listen to what He said. They would learn what He taught.

These men had learned the best way to God. Who knows the way better than God's Son?

WHAT DO YOU THINK?
What this story teaches: Who knows the way to God better than His Son? Follow Him!
1. Why do you think each man decided to follow Jesus? Why didn't they follow someone else?
2. Who is Jesus? If you want to find your way to God, who knows the way best? Why?

9

Muffkins on Parade!
A Muffin Make-believe Story

"Where are you going?" asked the Muffkin with the little tin horn.

"To see the king!" said the Muffkin with the booming drum.

"May I go, too?"

"Come on! We'll have a parade."

"Where are you going?" asked the Muffkin with the cymbals.

"To see the king!" said the Muffkins with the little tin horn and the booming drum.

"May I go, too?"

"Come on! We'll have a parade."

"Where are you going?" asked the Muffkin with the wooden baton.

"To see the king!" said the Muffkins with the cymbals, the little tin horn, and the booming drum.

"May I go, too?"

"Come on! We'll have a parade."

"Where are you going?" asked the Muffkin with the bright little flag.

"To see the king!" said the Muffkins with the wooden baton, the cymbals, the little tin horn, and the booming drum.

"May I go, too?"

"Come on! We'll have a parade."

"Where are you going?" asked the Muffkin with the little Ruffkin dog and Tuffkin cat.

"To see the king!" said the Muffkins with the bright little flag, the wooden baton, the cymbals, the little tin horn, and the booming drum.

"May I go, too?"

"Come on! We'll have a parade."

"Where are you going?" asked the king's son, who sat beside the road.

"To see the king!" said the Muffkins with the little Ruffkin dog and Tuffkin cat, the bright little flag, the wooden baton, the cymbals, the little tin horn, and the booming drum.

"Do you know how to get there?" asked the king's son.

"Of course!" they all said. "Do you want to join our parade?"

The king's son smiled. "I'm on my way home," he said. "Do you want to follow me?"

"Oh, no!" the other Muffkins said. "We're Muffkins on parade. We're on our way to see the king!"

The Muffkins on parade boomed the drum, tooted the horn, clanged the cymbals, twirled the baton, and waved the flag. They walked around and around a big tree. The little Ruffkin dog and Tuffkin cat walked around and around with them. It was quite something to see and hear!

The king's son watched by the side of the road. He watched the parade go around and around. But he saw that it was going nowhere, just around and around. It was certainly not going to see the king.

At last the king's son yawned. "I think they will never go to see the king," he said. "Perhaps they do not know the way."

Then the king's son got up and went home. There the king was waiting to have dinner with him.

LET'S TALK ABOUT THIS

What this story teaches: If you want to see the king, follow his son. If you want to see God, follow His Son, Jesus. Who knows the way except Him?

1. Where did the Muffkins on parade want to go? Did they know the way?

2. How do those Muffkins on parade remind you of people you know?

3. Do you know people who are going around in circles trying to find God by themselves?

4. Who is the only Person who knows the way to God? Since He knows the way to God, what should we do when He says, "Follow Me"?

5. Are you following Jesus? Have you ever accepted Him as your Savior and Lord? Would you like to?

Do It!

John 2:1-11

What is more exciting than a wedding? A wedding is a time for happiness and laughter. It is a time for family and friends. So it shouldn't surprise us to find Jesus at a wedding in the little village of Cana.

Two days had passed since Jesus had said, "Follow Me." Four men–Peter, Andrew, Philip, and Nathanael–followed Him. They went with Him wherever He went. They listened to Him teach and preach. They tried to learn all they could about God and heaven.

During those two days, Jesus had come back home to Galilee. He was just in time for a wedding at the little village of Cana, a few miles north of His hometown, Nazareth. Jesus, His mother, and His friends had been invited.

But something happened at this wedding. There must have been more people than they expected. Or perhaps the man in charge of the wedding had not been too careful. When the party was at its best, they ran out of wine.

"What will we do?" the man in charge must have moaned.

The man in charge must have told several people about his problem. He certainly told Mary, Jesus' mother. And she told Jesus. Mary even told Jesus that He should do something about it.

"But this isn't the time to be doing miracles," Jesus said to His mother.

Mary smiled. She must have known that Jesus would do something. Perhaps it *was* the time for miracles. Jesus may have said that to test how much she really believed in Him.

"Do exactly what He tells you to do!" Mary told the servants. That is good advice for anyone. When Jesus says, "Do this," we should do it!

The servants were ready. They had been trained to obey. So when Jesus said, "Do this," they did it.

"Fill those six stone pots with water," Jesus told them. They did exactly what He told them to do. Each of those large pots held about thirty gallons, so that was a lot of filling. They must have carried water until they wanted to complain. But they did exactly what He told them to do.

"Dip some from the water pots," Jesus told them. "Take it to the man in charge."

"Water?" they wondered. "Why take water to the man in charge? He wants wine for the wedding."

But they did exactly what Jesus told them to do. They dipped some of the water and took it to the man in charge. But when he tasted it, he smiled. This wasn't water at all. It was the best wine he had ever tasted.

"You've saved your best to the last," the man in charge told the bridegroom. "Most people serve their best first. This is a good idea!"

The bridegroom must have smiled, shrugged his shoulders, and looked puzzled about the whole thing. What was going on? He certainly didn't know. But Mary knew. And the servants knew. They must have stared at Jesus, talking happily with some wedding guests. He had done something that an ordinary man could never do. It was a miracle! It was the first miracle He had done before a crowd. But it would not be His last.

WHAT DO YOU THINK?
What this story teaches: Jesus can make wonderful things happen in your life. Obey Him!
1. Why do you think the servants obeyed Jesus? What would have happened if they had not?
2. Why should you obey your parents, your teachers, Jesus, and others God has sent to guide you? What may happen if you don't?

Wonderful Things
A Muffin Make-believe Story

"Listen to that noise!" the king's son said to himself.

He leaned out his open window and looked toward the village. There they were! The Muffkins on parade. They were going around and around the big tree again.

"Maybe they still want to see the king," the king's son said with a smile. "I will talk with them again."

The king's son left the palace where his father, the king, lived. He went across the drawbridge. He walked down the long hill to the village. Then he sat down on a big stump and watched the parade.

The Muffkin with the little tin horn tooted as loud as he could.

The Muffkin with the booming drum boomed with all of his might.

The Muffkin with the cymbals clanged and banged until the leaves on the tree quivered.

The Muffkin with the wooden baton twirled and whirled.

The Muffkin with the bright little flag waved it back and forth.

And the Muffkin with the little Ruffkin dog and Tuffkin cat followed behind.

The king's son liked the parade. He liked the Muffkins on parade. "But the music sounds awful," he said.

"Stop! Stop!" said the king's son. The tin horn stopped tooting. The big drum stopped booming. The cymbals stopped clanging and banging. The wooden baton stopped twirling. The flag stopped waving. And the little Ruffkin dog and the little Tuffkin cat stopped and watched to see what was happening.

"Do exactly what I tell you," the king's son told the Muffkins on parade. "Take this to the royal music store down the street."

The king's son wrote a note to the royal music store man. You can guess what it said. And you can guess what he told each Muffkin to do when he got to the royal music store.

Before long the Muffkin with the little tin horn came tooting down the street. But he didn't have a little tin horn now. He had a beautiful golden horn.

Then the Muffkin with the booming drum came booming down the street. But he didn't have the old drum he had before. He had a royal drum fit for a royal drummer.

Next came the Muffkin with the clanging, banging cymbals. But he didn't have clanging, banging cymbals now. Instead he had cymbals that went *"choing! sproing!"* like royal Muffkin cymbals do.

The Muffkin with the wooden baton was now the Muffkin with a beautiful baton. He twirled it as a royal baton twirler should.

The Muffkin with the bright little flag now had a royal flag to wave.

When the Muffkin with the golden horn marched with the Muffkin with the royal drum, and he marched with the Muffkin with the *"choing! sproing!"* royal Muffkin cymbals, the Muffkin with the beautiful baton marched, too. They all marched with their chins a little higher.

Even the little Ruffkin dog and the little Tuffkin cat marched behind the royal flag more proudly than they had before!

The king's son smiled. "Wonderful music!" he said.

"Thank you!" cheered the Muffkins on parade. "And thank you for the wonderful things! We're glad we did exactly what you told us to do!"

LET'S TALK ABOUT THIS

What this story teaches: Wonderful things come when you obey the right person.

1. What kind of music did the Muffkins make at first? What did the king's son tell them to do? Did they obey him exactly? How do you know?

2. What kind of music did they make then?

3. When parents want you to obey exactly, what should you do? When Jesus wants you to obey exactly, what should you do?

19

How Do I Get There?

John 3:1-21

"I must see Him!" Nicodemus whispered. "I must talk with Him!"

Nicodemus hurried along the dark streets of Jerusalem. The moon and stars lit his way. So did the olive oil lamps that flickered in the windows.

"I have never seen a man like Him before," Nicodemus whispered. "I have never seen anyone do the things He has done. I have never heard anyone say the things that He has said. I MUST find Him! I MUST talk with Him!"

Nicodemus hid whenever a person came along the street. He did not want anyone to see Him going to Jesus. He did not want anyone to know that he was going to ask Jesus about God and heaven.

Most of the people thought Nicodemus and his friends knew all about God. They thought that Nicodemus and his friends knew how to get to heaven. That was because Nicodemus and his friends pretended that they knew those things.

But Nicodemus was not so sure now. He had heard Jesus talk about God. He had heard Jesus tell about His home in heaven. Jesus was not pretending to know God. He was not pretending to know about heaven. Nicodemus was sure that Jesus had lived with God. He was sure that Jesus had lived in heaven.

"Could He be God's Son?" Nicodemus wondered. "I must ask Him. God's Son would know these things!"

Somehow Nicodemus knew where Jesus was staying. He knocked quietly on the courtyard gate. The man who owned the house answered.

"I MUST see Jesus," Nicodemus whispered.

"Upstairs, on the rooftop," the man answered. He pointed to an open stairway going up from the courtyard to the rooftop.

Nicodemus hurried up the stairs. Jesus was waiting for him. He had known that Nicodemus was coming. That is because Jesus knows all that is happening.

20

"God has sent You!" Nicodemus told Jesus. "Your miracles show that You have come from Him."

Jesus looked at Nicodemus. He knew that Nicodemus really wanted to ask, "How can I go to heaven?"

"You must be born again!" Jesus said. "That is the only way to heaven."

Nicodemus looked puzzled. "How?" he asked. "How can an older man like me go back into his mother and be born a second time?"

Jesus smiled. Nicodemus wasn't pretending now. He REALLY wanted to know.

"God's Spirit comes to you like the wind in the trees," said Jesus. He pointed to the wind blowing in the olive trees nearby. "You see the leaves move. You hear them rustle. So you know the wind is blowing because of the things it does. But you never see the wind."

Nicodemus listened carefully.

"You never see God's spirit," Jesus told Nicodemus. "But you see what He does in others."

"How?" Nicodemus asked again.

"You are the teacher, the religious leader," said Jesus. "Are you teaching about God and heaven before you understand?"

Nicodemus looked ashamed. That was exactly what he had been doing.

"Do you remember the bronze snake that Moses put on a pole in the wilderness?" Jesus asked.

Nicodemus remembered.

"I will be lifted up the same way. Everyone who believes in Me will live forever."

Nicodemus was quiet. He began to see more clearly now. Jesus WAS God's Son! He had come from heaven to tell people these things.

"God loved the world so much that He gave His only Son," Jesus told Nicodemus. "Whoever believes in God's Son will never die, but will live forever."

God's Son! Now Nicodemus was sure! Who else could tell him how to live forever in heaven?

The Bible does not tell us what Nicodemus did later that night. But he must have accepted Jesus as his Savior. Later, when Jesus was crucified, Nicodemus and another man asked for His body. Tenderly they wrapped it with spices. And they laid it in a tomb.

Nicodemus was not ashamed of Jesus then! He was not ashamed to let the whole world know that he was Jesus' friend. Are you?

WHAT DO YOU THINK?

What this story teaches: Who can tell you how to get somewhere? The person who has been there! Who can tell you how to get to heaven? Jesus, God's Son, for that is His home!

1. If you wanted to go to a certain place, would you ask a person who had been there, or a person who had never been there? Why?

2. Do you want to go to heaven some day? Who knows the way best? Why does He? Have you asked Him to show you the way? Would you like to now?

Follow Me!
A Muffin Make-believe Story

"Listen to our music now," said the Muffkin with the golden horn.

"It is wonderful music," said the Muffkin with the royal drum. "The prince said so."

"That is because he gave us wonderful instruments," said the Muffkin with the *"choing! sproing!"* cymbals.

"But now we should do something wonderful with our wonderful music," said the Muffkin with the beautiful baton. "But what?"

"Play for the king!" said the Muffkin with the little Ruffkin dog and the little Tuffkin cat.

"Now!" said the Muffkin with the royal flag.

It was such a good idea. Why hadn't they thought of it before?

"But how do we get there?" asked the Muffkins in a chorus. "Who knows the way?"

"I do," said the king's son. "Follow me."

The Muffkins looked at the prince. "How do you know the way?" one of them asked.

The prince smiled. "I know the way because...

   I am the king's son,

   I live in the king's home, and

   I have gone that way before."

The Muffkins on parade began to play their new instruments again. They began to march in parade. Then they all followed the prince toward the king's home. There they would play for the king.

But along the way they came to a fork in the road. One road went this way. The other road went that way.

"Follow me this way," said the prince.

But the Muffkin with the golden horn stopped playing. He looked this way. He looked that way.

"That way is a prettier way," he said. "Surely that way goes to the king's home."

"The king's home is THIS way," said the prince. "If you want to go there, you must follow me."

"Follow the prince!" said the other Muffkins on parade. So all the Muffkins began to play. And all of them followed the prince.

But before long they came to another fork in the road. The Muffkin with the royal drum stopped beating it.

"That way looks like an easier path to follow," he said. "Surely that way goes to the king's home."

"The king's home is THIS way," said the prince. 'If you want to go there, you must follow me."

"Follow the prince!" said the other Muffkins on parade. So all the Muffkins began to play. And all of them followed the prince.

Soon they came to another fork in the road. The Muffkin with the *"choing! sproing!"* cymbals stopped choinging and sproinging.

"That way looks like more fun," he said. "Surely that way goes to the king's home."

"The king's home is THIS way," said the prince. "If you want to go there, you must follow me."

"Follow the prince!" said the other Muffkins on parade. So all the Muffkins began to play. And all of them followed the prince.

At another fork in the road the Muffkin with the beautiful baton stopped twirling. He thought THIS WAY was wider. And he thought it was surely the way to the king's home. But all the other Muffkins said, "Follow the prince!" And they did.

At last the Muffkins on parade came to still another fork in the road. The Muffkin with the little Ruffkin dog and the little Tuffkin cat had a problem. The little Ruffkin dog wanted to go one way. The little Tuffkin cat wanted to go another way.

"Follow the prince!" said all the other Muffkins. So they did.

Suddenly the Muffkins on parade saw the castle. And almost as suddenly they marched across the drawbridge, tooting, booming, and making all kinds of wonderful music. At last the Muffkins on parade would play for the king.

"We are here!" said the Muffkin with the golden horn.

"We are at the king's home!" said the Muffkin with the royal drum.

"We found our way!" said the Muffkin with the "*choing! sproing!*" cymbals.

"Because we followed the prince!" said the Muffkin with the beautiful baton.

The Muffkin with the little Ruffkin dog and the little Tuffkin cat said nothing. He went to see the king.

LET'S TALK ABOUT THIS
What this story teaches: Are you trying to go somewhere? Follow the one who knows the way!
1. Where were the Muffkins trying to go? Why? Did they know the way themselves?
2. Who knew the way to the king? How did he know?
3. Whom did the Muffkins on parade follow? Where did he take them?
4. Who knows the way to God? How does Jesus know that? Will you follow Him?

Three Towns
Matthew 11:20-24

Would you like to have lived in the little fishing village of Bethsaida? If you had, you would have seen some wonderful things happen.

When Jesus was in this little village one day some people brought a blind man to Him. They felt sorry for the man. In those days blind people could not get a job. They had no way to earn money. So most of them sat in the streets and begged. Begging never brought much money, so blind people were also poor people.

No one could help this blind man to see. The best doctors in the land could not do that. But Jesus touched him, and the man saw! If you had seen Jesus do that, what would you have thought about Him? Would you have believed that He was God's Son? Of course you would!

But most of the people of Bethsaida didn't. After all, Jesus was only their neighbor who lived in Capernaum.

Another day, Jesus took five small loaves of bread and two fish into His hands. He kept breaking them until He had enough food to feed five thousand people!

That was on a quiet hill near Bethsaida. The people of Bethsaida saw Him. If you had seen Jesus do that, what would you have thought about Him? Would you have believed that He was God's Son? Of course you would!

But most of the people of Bethsaida didn't. After all, Jesus was only their neighbor who lived a few miles up the road.

"Woe to you, Bethsaida!" Jesus said. "If the people of Tyre and Sidon had seen these miracles, they would have turned from their sins and accepted Me." The people of Bethsaida were shocked. Tyre and Sidon were "foreign" cities. The people of Bethsaida thought they were right and the "foreign" cities were wrong.

But Jesus said that you must turn from your sins and accept Him. You must do that if you are a neighbor. And you must do that if you live far away in another land.

"Woe to you, Chorazin!" Jesus said later. Chorazin was another little village near Jesus' hometown, Capernaum. They had seen Jesus do many miracles. They knew that no man could do those things. Only God's Son could do them. But they refused to accept Him. He was just their neighbor from Capernaum.

"Woe to you, Capernaum!" Jesus said also. Capernaum was His hometown. He had moved there when the people of Nazareth had driven Him out. The people of Nazareth were angry when Jesus told them He was God's Son. The people of Capernaum let Jesus live there. They didn't drive Him out. They watched Him do one miracle after another. They saw Him do things that only God's Son could do. But most of them did not accept Him as their Savior. After all, He was only their hometown neighbor!

The three towns were so foolish! They had God's Son living among them. They saw Him do miracles that no one else could do. But they would not accept Him.

"Woe to you!" Jesus told them. Today those three towns are gone. Nothing is there but grassy hillsides and piles of stones.

WHAT DO YOU THINK?
What this story teaches: Jesus' miracles show that He is God's Son. Woe to anyone who refuses to accept Him.
1. What did each of the villages see Jesus do? Could anyone else do those miracles? So what did those miracles tell about Jesus?
2. What did Jesus say to each of the three towns? Why? What did they do wrong?

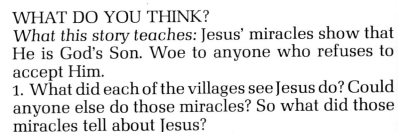

Clanging and Banging

A Muffin Make-believe Story

"We're going to play for the king!" said the Muffkin with the golden horn.

"But where is the king?" asked the Muffkin with the royal drum.

The king's son smiled. "He is in the royal music room," he said. "I have asked him to listen to your music. He has invited you to play for him!"

"Then we are important Muffkins!" shouted the Muffkin with the *"choing! sproing!"* cymbals. He thought he was so important that he began to go *"clang! bang!"* with his cymbals.

"We ARE important Muffkins!" shouted the Muffkin with the beautiful baton. He began to twirl his beautiful baton in a silly new way.

"Yes WE are important Muffkins!" shouted the Muffkin with the royal drum. He began to bang on his drum. Instead of the nice *"boom! boom!"* it went *"clomp! whomp!"*

"We really are IMPORTANT Muffkins!" shouted the Muffkin with the golden horn. Instead of the nice "*toot! toot!*" he began to play a strange sounding "*honk! honk!*"

"Stop! Stop!" said the prince. "That is not wonderful music. The king will not like it!"

But the Muffkins liked it. They thought it made them sound important.

So the Muffkins on parade went marching into the royal music room. They were clanging, banging, clomping, whomping, honking, and twirling in a silly new way.

"Stop! Stop!" the prince kept shouting. "This is wrong! The king will not like it!"

The Muffkins on parade knew that their clanging and banging and clomping and whomping and honking and twirling was wrong. But they kept on doing it anyway. They thought it made them sound important.

When the king heard them, he put his hands over his ears. "Stop! Stop!" he shouted. "That is not wonderful music! It is clanging and banging and clomping and whomping and honking and twirling the wrong way."

But the Muffkins on parade kept on with the music they wanted. They thought it made them sound important.

"Stop! Stop!" the king shouted again. "I want to hear the wonderful music!"

But the Muffkins on parade did not play the wonderful music. They kept on with their clanging and banging and clomping and whomping and honking and twirling the wrong way.

"Out! Out!" shouted the king. "Get that noisy parade out of here!"

Before the Muffkins on parade could play one more sour note, the royal guards marched them out of the royal music room. They marched them right out of the castle.

Now the Muffkins on parade knew how foolish they had been. They had not pleased the king. So now they could not play their wonderful music for him.

LET'S TALK ABOUT THIS

What this story teaches: When you know what is right, but don't do it, you're headed for trouble.

1. What did the Muffkins on parade do wrong when they played for the king? Why did they do that?
2. What should the Muffkins have done? What happened to them when they did not?
3. What did you learn about YOU from this story? What will it help you to do?

DARE TO BE A DANIEL

Don't Touch That!
Daniel 1

"What will happen to us?" Daniel and his friends wondered.

The four friends felt sad and lonely. They had seen King Nebuchadnezzar's soldiers burn their beautiful city Jerusalem. They had seen those soldiers kill many of their friends and neighbors.

Some of the strongest and best of the people had been captured. Now they were forced to march far away from home. They were going to Babylon. But nobody knew what would happen to them there.

Would they be prisoners in a dark, lonely jail? Would they be slaves, forced to work hard in the hot sunlight? Or would they be tortured?

One day Daniel and his friends were surprised. A Babylonian officer named Ashpenaz came to see them. He was friendly. He even smiled at them.

"You four young men will have an important job here in Babylon," he told them. "You will go to the best schools. You will learn to be officers. You will work for the king. You may even become some of the most important men in Babylon."

That certainly seemed to be good news. Any young man should want a job like that.

But Daniel and his friends wondered. What would they have to do for the king? Could they please him and God at the same time? What if the king wanted something and God did not want them to do it?

36

The four friends must have worried a little when their names were changed. The new names were Babylonian. They would no longer be called by their Hebrew names.

But they worried even more when they learned what they would eat. It was the same food and wine given to the king. Should they eat it? Some was pork, and God had commanded the Hebrews not to eat the meat of pigs. Most of it had probably been offered to idols. God's people certainly should not eat that. And they did not want to drink the king's wine, either.

Should they just eat the food and not make a fuss about it? Or should they decide that they would not eat it and tell the king's officer Ashpenaz?

Daniel made up his mind. He would not eat the king's food or drink his wine. The other three decided they would be like Daniel.

Daniel talked with Ashpenaz about it. As nicely as he could, he asked Ashpenaz to give them other good food instead.

Ashpenaz liked Daniel. He wanted to help. But he was worried.

"What if your food makes you thinner than the other men?" he asked. "The king will cut off my head!"

"May we try it for ten days?" Daniel asked.

That seemed fair enough. Ten days couldn't hurt very much. So Ashpenaz gave Daniel and his friends other food for ten days.

Daniel and his friends did not get thinner. They were even healthier than the other men. How happy Ashpenaz was. But Daniel and his friends were happier. They had decided to please God, no matter what happened. Now they knew that God was with them. He would take care of them, for they had been faithful to Him.

WHAT DO YOU THINK?

What this story teaches: Does God want you to do something? Then do it! Does He want you to stay away from something? Then don't touch it!

1. Why did Daniel and his friends decide not to eat the king's food? Whom were they trying to please most?

2. Can you think of some things God does not want you to do? What should you do about them?

"No!"
A Muffin Family Story

Maxi was still thinking about the Sunday school lesson when he went to school on Monday morning. They had talked about Daniel and his friends. They had talked about the way Daniel had refused the king's wine. He had refused to eat the king's meat. It had been an offering for idols.

"So what does that have to do with us?" Pookie had asked. "No king is going to offer wine to us kids. And not too many hamburgers have been offered to idols first."

The other kids in the class thought Pookie had a good point. Maxi was still wondering about that as he walked to school.

He certainly didn't expect a king to offer him wine at school. And he certainly didn't expect to find a hamburger that had been offered to an idol.

"So what?" Maxi almost said aloud.

When classes began, Maxi was too busy to think about Daniel and the king's food. And when lunch time came he was too busy thinking about his own food. So by the time school was over that day, Maxi had forgotten about Daniel.

Maxi came out of the door of the school and headed down the sidewalk toward home. Then he heard someone whisper his name.

"Psssst! Maxi!"

Maxi looked. There were three of his school friends. They were standing by a clump of bushes.

"Come here!" they whispered. "We've got something to show you."

Maxi walked over to the bushes. One of the boys pulled a bright package from his pocket.

"Look what I've got," he said. "We're going behind the bushes for a smoke. Come on!"

Maxi's heart began to pound. He had never done that before. Something inside said, "Go on! It will be fun!"

Suddenly Maxi seemed to see Mommi's and Poppi's smiling faces. He knew they would not want him to do this.

"Sorry, fellows," said Maxi. He turned to leave.

"Sissy!" said one of the friends. Maxi bristled.

"Are you a little boy or a man?" asked another.

Maxi took a step back toward his friends. His heart began to pound again. Maybe just once wouldn't hurt.

Suddenly Maxi seemed to see Mini's smiling face. He knew she would not want him to do this.

"Sorry, fellows," said Maxi. He turned to leave again.

"He's a little boy, not a man," said one of the other boys. "He's tied to his mommi's apron strings!"

Maxi bristled. He took a step back toward his friends. He looked at the package one was holding. What would it hurt to try this just once?

Suddenly Maxi seemed to see Daniel, refusing the king's wine and meat. Then he knew what the story of Daniel meant. Daniel had not done those things because God did not want him to do them. Then Maxi seemed to see Jesus' picture that hung on his bedroom wall. He knew that Jesus would not want him to do this.

"Sorry, fellows!" said Maxi. This time he walked straight home.

LET'S TALK ABOUT THIS

What this story teaches: Does God want you to do something? Then do it! Does He want you NOT to do it? Then don't!

1. What was Maxi tempted to do? Why do you think he thought about doing it? Have your friends ever tried to get you to do something you shouldn't?

2. Why didn't Maxi smoke with his friends? What kept him from doing it? What should you do the next time some friends want you to do something wrong?

Use It or Lose It!
Daniel 5

A new king ruled over Babylon. The old king, Nebuchadnezzar, had known Daniel and loved him. He had seen how God did many things through Daniel. He had known that God was with Daniel.

But this new king Belshazzar didn't care about Daniel or his God. He didn't seem to care about the old king, either. Actually, he didn't seem to care about anyone except Belshazzar. This new king wanted to have fun, no matter what it did to others.

One night Belshazzar had a big party. All the important people of the land were there. That is, all the important people who liked that kind of party. Daniel stayed home. He probably wasn't even invited.

Through the evening Belshazzar and his thousand guests drank wine. The party became wild and noisy as the king and his friends became drunk. They sang. They danced. They did everything they could think of doing to have fun.

Late that night the king became bored with all the drinking and singing and dancing. He wanted to do something exciting, something different. But what?

Then someone remembered the gold and silver cups that Nebuchadnezzar had taken from God's Temple in Jerusalem. Why not drink wine from them?

Belshazzar thought it was a great idea. The cups were brought, and wine was poured into them. As the king and his friends drank, they laughed at God. They praised the gods of Babylon and made fun of the God who had made them.

But suddenly the king turned pale. He was so frightened that his knees knocked together. With a trembling hand, he pointed to the wall. A giant hand was silently writing something.

People screamed and shouted. Others trembled in fear.

"What is it?" the king cried out. "What is it writing?" But not one person at the party knew.

The astrologers and magicians were brought in. But they didn't know, either. By this time the king was terrified. He offered a royal robe, a gold chain, and the third most important job in his kingdom to anyone who could read the writing.

The queen, who had not been at the party, came to see the king. She had heard what had happened and had a suggestion.

"Don't be afraid," she told the king. "Daniel can tell you what this says. He can even tell you what it means!"

Daniel was brought in a hurry. The king offered him the same rich gifts.

"You may keep your gifts," said Daniel. "But I will tell you what this means. God gave you this land. He made you king. He gave you riches. But you have not used those things for Him. You have turned against Him and have made fun of Him."

The king listened carefully to every word Daniel told him. "God will now take those things from you," Daniel said. "Your kingdom will be given to others."

The king did not like what he heard. But he gave Daniel the royal robe, gold chain, and third best job as he had promised.

That night the army of Darius the Mede broke into the city. Belshazzar was killed. God gave his kingdom to others, just as Daniel had said.

WHAT DO YOU THINK?
What this story teaches: Use God's gifts for Him, or you may lose them.
1. What had God given to King Belshazzar? How did he use those gifts? Was God pleased? Why not?
2. What did God do with the gifts He had given to Belshazzar? Why do you think He did that?

44

Scrumptious Strawberry Pie
A Muffin Family Story

"Mommi, Mommi! Doesn't this recipe look DE-licious?" Mini asked with a big smile.

Mommi smiled too. The recipe was called "Scrumptious Strawberry Pie." The picture showed a beautiful pie with strawberries sticking out of it. It had a frilly cream topping. Mommi thought it looked DE-licious too.

Mini thumbed through the rest of the pages of the magazine. Then she came back to the scrumptious strawberry pie.

"May I?" Mini asked.

Mommi looked up from the cookies she was making. "May I what?" she asked.

"May I make this scrumptious strawberry pie?" Mini asked.

"That would be fun," said Mommi. "When should we do it?"

Mini was quiet for a moment. "Mommi, I'd like to make this pie all by myself. OK?"

Now Mommi was quiet for a moment. She looked carefully at the scrumptious strawberry pie recipe.

"It's not an easy recipe," said Mommi. "But if you want to try, OK."

The next day Mommi came from the grocery store with a beautiful box of strawberries. They were just like the beautiful red strawberries Mini saw in the magazine.

"I bought these just for you," said Mommi. "They are especially for your scrumptious strawberry pie."

"Oh, thank you, thank you," said Mini. "They are just be-YOO-tiful."

"They are also very ripe," said Mommi. "That means you must make your scrumptious strawberry pie soon."

"I will, I will!" said Mini. "But please don't say another word about it. I want to do this all by myself."

"All right, Mini, I will not say one more word about it," Mommi promised. And she didn't.

That afternoon Mini went to the park for a swim at the pool. The next morning she and Maxi played in the treehouse. After lunch she colored in her coloring book. Then came dinner, and dishes, and a game with Maxi before bedtime.

The next day went about the same way. So did the next and the next. Mini had almost forgotten about the scrumptious strawberry pie. She had almost forgotten until she opened the refrigerator to get some milk.

Suddenly Mini saw the strawberries sitting on the top shelf. Then she looked at them a second time. They were not bright red now. Instead they were a dark red box of mooshy moldy mess.

Mini let out a little cry, and Mommi came running. "Oh, Mommi, Mommi," Mini said. "They were SO beautiful! Now look at them. And you bought them especially for me. Why didn't you tell me they were rotting?"

"Because I promised I would not say one more word about the pie," said Mommi. "Remember?"

Mini did remember. She felt sad now. Mommi had given her a beautiful box of strawberries. Now they were a mooshy moldy mess.

That night Poppi read the story about Daniel and King Belshazzar. Then he read what the story teaches, "Use God's gifts for Him, or you may lose them."

Mini jumped when Poppi read that. "That's just like the strawberries Mommi bought me," she said. "I didn't use them, so I lost them."

"And that's just like the gifts God gives us," said Poppi. "We must use them for Him or lose them."

"Then I learned more from the mooshy moldy mess than from the scrumptious strawberry pie!" said Mini.

LET'S TALK ABOUT THIS

What this story teaches: God gives us many good things. Use them for Him or you may lose them.
1. What did Mommi give to Mini? Did she use Mommi's gift the way she should? What happened to the gift?
2. How did this story remind you of Daniel and King Belshazzar? What did you learn from it?

Keep Praying!

Daniel 6

When Darius the Mede began to rule, he put three presidents over the land. Daniel was one of them. The other two presidents did not like Daniel. He was a foreigner. He was also a better ruler than they, and they were afraid he would be put over them.

Those two jealous men began to look for some way to get Daniel in trouble. But Daniel did everything right. They could find nothing wrong.

"I know!" one said. "He prays."

"So what?" asked the other.

"So we will make a law against praying!"

The two jealous men went to the king. "All of the important people in the land want a new law," they told the king.

"What new law?" asked the king.

"Nobody can ask a special favor of God or man except from you," they said. "This law will be for thirty days."

The king felt good about the new law. Just think! He would be the only one in the kingdom who could give a special favor! So he signed the law.

Daniel always prayed each day. He did it a certain way, and the two jealous men knew it. Each day he prayed three times in his upstairs bedroom, with his windows open toward Jerusalem. People on the street below could see him praying through the open window.

Now there was a law against praying! What would Daniel do? If he stopped praying, the people would think the king was more important than God to Daniel. If he prayed, the two jealous men would have Daniel thrown into a den of hungry lions. That was the way people were executed!

The jealous men ran to Daniel's house and waited to see what he would do. They didn't have long to wait. Daniel opened his windows. He knelt down and prayed.

The men rushed to the king. "Didn't you sign a new law against praying?" they asked. "And doesn't a person who breaks this law get thrown into a den of lions?"

"Yes, that's the law," said the king. "It must not be broken. Even I can't change the law."

"Then you must throw Daniel into the den of lions," the wicked men said. "We caught him praying."

Now the king was sad. He liked Daniel very much. He liked Daniel much more than the two men!

But as the king said, even he could not change the law. So he had to throw Daniel into a den of hungry lions.

"I hope the God to whom you pray will keep you safe," the king told Daniel. Then a stone was put over the opening. A mark was made so that nobody could roll the stone away without breaking the mark.

That night the king refused to go to bed. He waited anxiously for morning to come. When it did, he rushed to the lions' den.

"Daniel! Did your God protect you from the lions?" the king called out.

"Yes! He shut the mouths of the lions," Daniel answered. "This should show that I did nothing wrong."

The king was so happy. Then he gave another order: "From now on, the people of this kingdom must honor Daniel's God, for He is really God."

Of course, Daniel kept on praying each day!

WHAT DO YOU THINK?

What this story teaches: Keep on praying, no matter what happens.

1. Why did the two jealous men want Daniel killed? What was their plan to get rid of him?

2. How did the king feel about putting Daniel in the lions' den? How did God take care of Daniel?

3. What did you learn about praying? Will you keep on praying?

Maxi and the Lions
A Muffin Family Story

"Daniel was certainly brave," said Maxi. Poppi had just read about Daniel and the lions' den. "I'm glad we aren't thrown to some lions today because we pray."

"Me, too," said Mini. "We put on our nice clothes and go to church and Sunday school, and nobody bothers us."

"It hasn't always been that way," said Poppi. "Many of our great-great-great grandmommis and grandpoppis were killed. Some people didn't like the way they worshiped God."

"Were they thrown to the lions?" asked Mini.

Poppi laughed. "No lions then," he said. "But they were just as brave as Daniel."

Maxi was still thinking about Daniel and the lions when he went to bed. He looked up at the picture of Jesus on his wall. Then he thought about the great-great-great grandmommis and grandpoppis who were as brave as Daniel.

Maxi could still see that picture of Daniel in the lions' den. The picture was still there as he drifted off to sleep.

But suddenly the lions in the picture began to move. They came toward Maxi. Then he saw that Daniel was gone. He was there alone with the lions.

Then something else happened. The walls of the lions' den began to change. The lions' den was no longer the lions' den. It was Maxi's own church.

Some of Maxi's friends were trying to get into the church. But one of the lions sat on the front steps. He roared and growled and would not let them in.

"I'll be as brave as Daniel!" Maxi said in his dream. Then he chased the lion away, with all of his friends helping.

Maxi and his friends went toward their Sunday school room. But they found another lion sitting in the doorway. The lion roared and growled and would not let them in.

"I'll be as brave as Daniel!" Maxi said in his dream. Then he chased the lion away, with all of his friends helping.

Maxi tiptoed toward the room where the preacher preached to them. But another lion was in the doorway. Mommis and poppis were trying to get in. But the lion would not let them. He roared and growled.

"I'll be as brave as Daniel!" Maxi said in his dream. Then he chased the lion away, with all of his friends helping.

"I WAS as brave as Daniel!" Maxi thought. But even as he said that, he felt someone tapping him gently on his shoulder. He looked around. Was it another lion?

But Maxi did not see another lion. He did not even see his friends now. All he saw was Mommi's smiling face, looking down on his.

Maxi looked this way. He looked that way. He saw now that he was safe in his own bed. It was all a dream.

"There was certainly a lot of roaring and growling in here," Mommi whispered. "Want to tell me about it?"

"Sure," said Maxi. "But don't think I'm LION about it." Then Maxi told Mommi about the lions at church.

"I'm glad we don't have to fight lions to go to church and Sunday school," said Maxi.

"Me, too!" said Mommi.

LET'S TALK ABOUT THIS

What this story teaches: It's good that we don't have to be as brave as Daniel to go to church and Sunday school. But we would be brave if we had to, wouldn't we?

1. What would you think if you had to fight lions to go to church and Sunday school? Aren't you glad you don't?

2. Do you ever thank God that you can go to His house on Sunday? Do you ever thank Him that you can pray and read your Bible without someone hurting you? Would you like to thank Him now?

GOOD HELPERS

Timothy-A Good Helper

Acts 16:1-4; 1 & 2 Timothy

Paul watched a handsome young man talking with some people nearby.

"Who is he?" asked Paul.

"Timothy," some friends answered.

"Timothy? The name sounds Greek," said Paul. "Is he Greek?"

The friends smiled. "His father is Greek, but his mother is Jewish," they answered. "You should meet that woman. Eunice has read the Scriptures and prayed with Timothy since he was a baby. So has Timothy's grandmother Lois."

Paul did meet Eunice and Lois. While he was there at Lystra, he met many of their friends, too. He told those people about Jesus. He told them about how Jesus was the Messiah, God's Son. He told them that Jesus died for them and wanted to be their Savior.

Eunice and Lois accepted Jesus as their Savior. So did Timothy. And so did many others at Lystra.

The next time Paul came to Lystra his friends began to tell him about Timothy. They told how Timothy had been working for Jesus there at Lystra.

"I need someone like Timothy to go with me," said Paul. "What a helper he would be!"

"Why don't you ask him?" said the friends.

So Paul asked Timothy to go with him. He asked Timothy to help him work for Jesus. But he warned Timothy that it would not be easy.

"People do not always like what I am saying," Paul told him. "Many do not want me to tell about Jesus. Some try to hurt me. Others try to kill me. Do you still want to go?"

"Of course," said Timothy. He wanted to work for Jesus. He would go anywhere. He would do whatever Jesus wanted, even if he got hurt.

Timothy went many places with Paul. He helped Paul work for Jesus.

"What a helper," Paul often said.

Sometimes Paul sent Timothy to a faraway city. Sometimes he told Timothy to stay while he went far away.

One time Paul and Timothy worked together at Ephesus. Later, Paul left for Rome, but asked Timothy to stay behind. When Paul reached Rome he wrote to Timothy.

Some time later, Timothy got another letter from Paul. In it Paul told him that he had been put into prison in Rome. He told Timothy that he might be put to death there.

"I pray for you every day," Paul wrote. "I want to see you very much. I know how you trust the Lord as your mother, Eunice, and grandmother Lois do. Please come to see me and bring my cloak and books."

Timothy must have hurried to Rome to see Paul. He must have taken Paul's cloak and books.

"What a good helper you are!" Paul told him.

And he was!

WHAT DO YOU THINK?

What this story teaches: We should try to be good helpers for Jesus.

1. How was Timothy a good helper for Jesus? How did he help Paul work for Jesus?

2. How did Timothy's mother and grandmother help him? Do you think that helped him become a good helper for Jesus later?

3. Paul's two letters to Timothy are found in the Bible. They are called 1 Timothy and 2 Timothy. Be sure to read 2 Timothy 1:5 and 2:2.

A Toot and a Boom for the Prince
A Muffin Make-believe Story

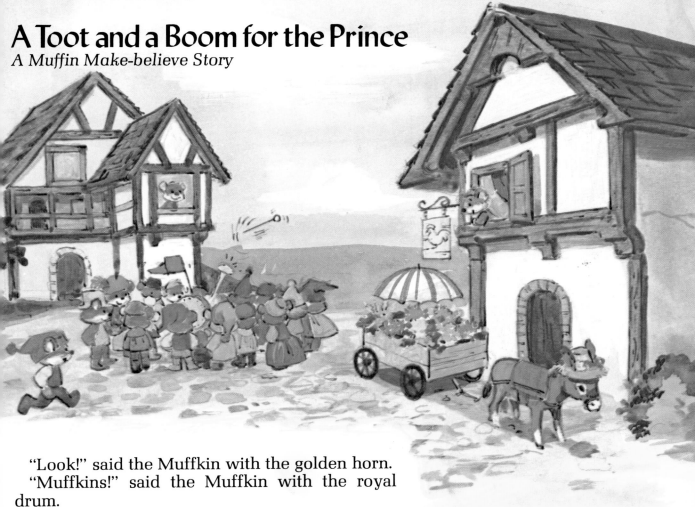

"Look!" said the Muffkin with the golden horn.

"Muffkins!" said the Muffkin with the royal drum.

"And they have all come here!" said the Muffkin with the beautiful baton.

"To listen to us!" said the Muffkin with the *"choing! sproing!"* cymbals.

"Play wonderful music," said the Muffkin with the royal flag. He waved it faster as he said that.

"And march in the parade!" said the Muffkin with the little Ruffkin dog and the little Tuffkin cat.

The Muffkins on parade tooted and boomed, they waved the baton and the flag, and they went *"choing! sproing!"* with the cymbals. The Muffkins who had come to listen clapped and cheered. They thought it was wonderful music.

The more the Muffkin crowd clapped and cheered, the more the Muffkins on parade played. They tooted, boomed, waved, and went *"choing! sproing!"* At last, they were too tired to play another note.

59

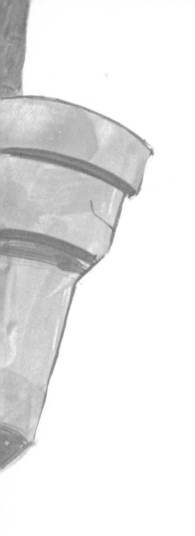

The Muffkin crowd went home. The Muffkins on parade got ready to go home, too. But someone came to see them. He had news, but it was not good news.

"The prince is not feeling well today," he said.

"We're sorry," said one of the Muffkins on parade. "What can we do?"

"He would like to hear some of your wonderful music," said the Muffkin. "That would cheer him more than anything."

The Muffkins on parade were so tired. They had tooted and boomed until they thought they could not give one more "*toot!*" or "*boom!*"

"But the prince," said the Muffkin with the golden horn.

"Is our friend," said the Muffkin with the royal drum.

"He gave us our instruments," said the Muffkin with the beautiful baton.

"So we MUST go to play for him," said the Muffkin with the "*choing! sproing!*" cymbals.

The Muffkins on parade picked up their instruments. They walked slowly up the hill toward the castle. When they came to the drawbridge, they began to toot and boom and wave and choing sproing.

Before long they saw the prince on his balcony. He waved to the Muffkins on parade.

"Wonderful music!" the prince called out to the Muffkins on parade.

The Muffkins on parade didn't feel tired any more. They were tooting and booming at their very best. And they tooted and boomed right up under the prince's balcony.

"Wonderful friends!" the prince called to them. "Thank you for coming. Wonderful friends are wonderful helpers, for you cheer me and help me get well soon."

LET'S TALK ABOUT THIS

What this story teaches: Good helpers will do good things, even when they are tired or don't want to.
1. Why were the Muffkins on parade good helpers? How were they like Timothy?
2. Think of some way you have been a good helper for your parents. Think of a way you could have been a good helper but weren't. Which was more fun?
3. What will you try to be this next week?

Eutychus-A Sleepy Listener

Acts 20:6-12

"Are you going to hear Paul tonight?"

"Of course. Every believer in Troas will be there!"

Paul had been in Troas all that week. He had arrived after a long trip through Macedonia, telling people about Jesus.

Each night that week Paul had preached to the people. This meeting would be the last before he would go on to Jerusalem. Every believer in Troas certainly would be there.

That Sunday afternoon some of Paul's friends began to prepare the room where he would preach. They set many olive oil lamps around the room. When the service was ready to begin, the lamps would be lit. The room would be filled with the bright yellow light.

Since this would be a communion service, the friends prepared the bread and wine. They made sure the room was clean and neat.

At last it was time for the people to gather. They began to come from all over Troas. They walked happily up the stairway to the third floor where the service would be held.

One by one the olive oil lamps were lit. The room glowed with the flickering light.

Before long the room was filled with people. Some of the young men gave up their places and sat in the open windows.

"Be careful!" some mothers whispered.

The young men smiled. Of course they would be careful. Their mothers should not worry.

Paul began to preach, and everyone listened. They could not often hear such a great preacher. No one whispered. No one went home.

But Paul kept on preaching for a long time. He kept on preaching until midnight.

Eutychus, one of the young men sitting in the windows, yawned. Then his head nodded. Eutychus caught himself falling asleep. He looked around. No one had seen him. But before long he yawned and nodded again and began to fall asleep. That happened two or three times. At last Eutychus could stay awake no longer. He fell asleep.

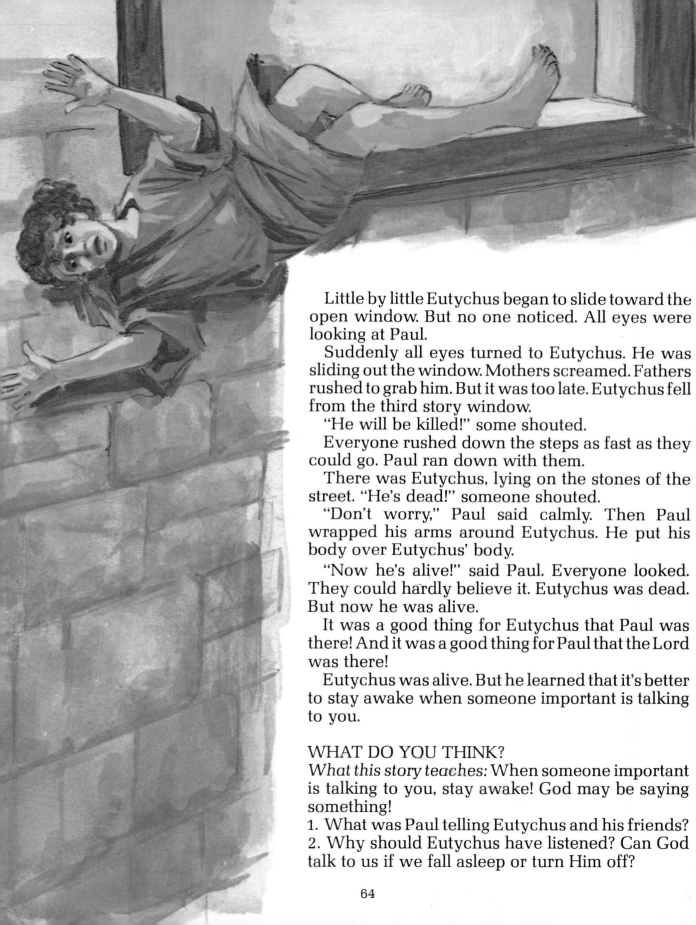

Little by little Eutychus began to slide toward the open window. But no one noticed. All eyes were looking at Paul.

Suddenly all eyes turned to Eutychus. He was sliding out the window. Mothers screamed. Fathers rushed to grab him. But it was too late. Eutychus fell from the third story window.

"He will be killed!" some shouted.

Everyone rushed down the steps as fast as they could go. Paul ran down with them.

There was Eutychus, lying on the stones of the street. "He's dead!" someone shouted.

"Don't worry," Paul said calmly. Then Paul wrapped his arms around Eutychus. He put his body over Eutychus' body.

"Now he's alive!" said Paul. Everyone looked. They could hardly believe it. Eutychus was dead. But now he was alive.

It was a good thing for Eutychus that Paul was there! And it was a good thing for Paul that the Lord was there!

Eutychus was alive. But he learned that it's better to stay awake when someone important is talking to you.

WHAT DO YOU THINK?
What this story teaches: When someone important is talking to you, stay awake! God may be saying something!
1. What was Paul telling Eutychus and his friends?
2. Why should Eutychus have listened? Can God talk to us if we fall asleep or turn Him off?

Royal Treasure Hunt

A Muffin Make-believe Story

"The king is coming! The king is coming!" a messenger said.

The Muffkins on parade stopped playing their horns and drums and things. They listened to the messenger.

"The king is coming here to the village," the messenger told them. "He is having a treasure hunt. You will be part of it."

That was exciting news. The Muffkins on parade tooted and boomed with excitement. They tooted and boomed until the king came. Then they were quiet. They wanted to listen to the king.

But the Muffkins on parade had tooted and boomed so much that they were tired and sleepy. When the king began to talk about the treasure hunt, their eyelids began to droop.

The king talked about the box of treasure he had hidden. He talked about the rules of the game. He told who could play the game and how they could win. Then he told several clues to help the Muffkins find the treasure.

65

But there was only one problem. While the king was telling about the box of treasure, the Muffkin with the golden horn fell asleep.

While the king talked about the way the box of treasure was hidden, the Muffkin with the royal drum fell asleep. And while the king talked about the rules of the game, the Muffkin with the beautiful baton fell asleep.

The Muffkin with the *"choing! sproing!"* cymbals fell asleep while the king told how the Muffkins could find the treasure. The Muffkin with the royal flag fell asleep when the king told the first clues. And the Muffkin with the Ruffkin dog and Tuffkin cat fell asleep when the king told the last clues.

Only the little Ruffkin dog and little Tuffkin cat stayed awake. Oh, of course, the king was awake, too. But he was not too happy when he saw all the snoozing, snoring Muffkins.

"The treasure hunt will begin!" said the king. "On your marks, get set, GO!"

The king said "GO" so loud that everyone woke up. "Go where?" asked the first Muffkin.

"On the treasure hunt," said the second.

"How?" asked the third.

"By following the king's rules and clues," said the fourth.

"WHAT rules and clues?" the Muffkins all asked together. Then they knew they had slept through different parts of the king's rules and clues. Only the little Ruffkin dog and Tuffkin cat had heard the last clues.

The Muffkins on parade started out on the treasure hunt. The first Muffkin could go only as far as he had listened. The second went farther, but soon he had to stop. Then the third, and the fourth, until all of the Muffkins had stopped the treasure hunt.

But the little Ruffkin dog and the little Tuffkin cat went on the last clues. And guess what? They found the treasure.

"The treasure is theirs!" said the king. "They will have a lifetime supply of royal dog food and royal cat food."

Of course all the Muffkins were sorry now that they hadn't listened. They were sorry they had fallen asleep when the king was talking to them.

LET'S TALK ABOUT THIS

What this story teaches: When someone is telling you something important, listen!

1. What happened to the Muffkins while the king was telling them something important? Why?

2. Do your parents ever tell you important things? Do your teachers? Does your pastor? Do others? What are some of the most important things those people have told you?

3. When they tell you important things, what should you do? Listen! Don't fall asleep. But don't tune them out or turn them off, either.

Onesimus-A Faithful Helper

Philemon

In Bible times many people owned slaves. They bought them and sold them as people would buy and sell horses and cattle.

Some people were cruel to their slaves. Others were kind. But even though a slave was treated kindly, he was still a slave.

One of Paul's friends, Philemon, owned a slave named Onesimus. Nobody knows why, but Onesimus ran away from Philemon. He went far away to Rome.

Somehow in that big city, Onesimus met Paul. Paul was in prison, with chains on his hands. But Paul still told people about Jesus. He told them about how Jesus could forgive them and be their Savior.

Onesimus listened carefully. He wanted Jesus to forgive his sins. He wanted a Savior and a Friend. So he accepted Jesus as his Savior. He knew then that Jesus was his Friend.

Many people would stay away from friends in prison. What if they would be thrown into prison too? But Onesimus did not stay away from Paul. He kept on coming to the prison to see him. He listened carefully as Paul taught him each day from God's Word.

Onesimus ran errands for Paul. He was a good helper, always willing to do something for his friend in prison. He was always willing to do something for his Friend Jesus.

Paul and Onesimus became good friends. They prayed together. They read God's Word together. They talked together about Jesus. They worked together for Him.

One day Onesimus came to the prison. He looked sad. "I must tell you something," he confessed. "I am a runaway slave. Will you still be my friend?"

"Of course!" Paul said, smiling. Haven't you been my friend, even though I'm in prison? But who is your master?"

"Philemon," Onesimus answered.

"Philemon?" Paul was startled. "He's my friend! I helped him learn God's Word, just as I did for you. And I helped him accept Jesus as his Savior too."

Now Onesimus felt even more sad. "What should we do?" he asked. "I want to do what is right. Should I go back and be his slave again?"

Paul was quiet. "What should I do?" he wondered. "I have TWO friends—a slave and his master. What SHOULD I do?"

Suddenly Paul knew what he must do. "Bring me a pen and a small scroll," he told Onesimus. "I will write a letter."

Onesimus brought the pen and the scroll. There in the prison in Rome, Paul wrote the letter to his friend Philemon. That letter is in your Bible and is called "Philemon."

"I always thank my God as I remember you in my prayers," Paul told his friend. "I'm asking you for my friend Onesimus. He is my dear friend and helper. Please accept him back as a friend, not as a slave."

Philemon loved Paul as a friend. Onesimus loved Paul as a friend. And Paul loved both of those men as his friends. Of course, all three loved Jesus as their Friend.

Philemon must have welcomed Onesimus home with open arms. "My friend," he said. "Welcome home!"

What a faithful helper Onesimus had been to Paul. Now he would be a faithful helper and friend to Philemon.

WHAT DO YOU THINK?
What this story teaches: Jesus' friends are faithful helpers. You can depend on them to do their best for Jesus—and you.
1. How did Onesimus help Paul? What kind of helper was he? Why?
2. When Onesimus left Philemon, he was a slave. When he came back, he was a friend and helper. What made the difference?
3. Are you a faithful helper for Jesus? Do you want to be?

Why?

A Muffin Make-believe Story

"Why?" BoBo Muffkin grumbled. "Why does Tony Muffkin treat me like a servant?"

BoBo Muffkin set the hamburger in front of Tony Muffkin. He felt like a servant. Whenever Tony Muffkin said, "do this," BoBo Muffkin did it. Whenever Tony Muffkin said, "do that," BoBo Muffkin did that too.

"Why?" he often asked himself.

It was a good question. But nobody answered it. Tony Muffkin never answered it. But that was because BoBo Muffkin never asked him. And, of course, how could BoBo Muffkin answer his own question? It wouldn't be a question if he had the answer when he asked it!

71

One day BoBo Muffkin stopped grumbling. He stopped doing things for Tony Muffkin. He went for a long walk.

"Why?" he kept asking.

"Why *what?*" a voice answered.

BoBo Muffkin looked around. There was his friend Maxi Muffkin.

"Why does Tony Muffkin treat me like a servant instead of a friend?" said BoBo Muffkin.

"How do you want him to treat you?" asked Maxi Muffkin.

"Like a friend instead of a servant," said BoBo Muffkin. "You always treat me like a friend. You never expect me to be a servant for you."

"But you always do nice things for me," said Maxi Muffkin.

"And you always do nice things for me, too," said BoBo Muffkin.

"Then good friends do good things for each other," said Maxi Muffkin. "Right?"

"Right!" said BoBo Muffkin. "But Tony Muffkin never does anything for me. He acts like I'm a servant instead of a friend."

Maxi Muffkin thought for a moment. "How do you treat Tony Muffkin?" he asked. "Like a friend or a servant?"

"I...I..." BoBo Muffkin tried to answer. He suddenly knew that he was not treating Tony Muffkin like a friend or a servant. He was treating him like a master. He was letting Tony Muffkin treat him like a servant.

"Did you answer your question?" asked Maxi Muffkin.

"Yes, but what can I do about it?" said BoBo Muffkin.

"Let's go talk to Tony Muffkin," Maxi Muffkin suggested.

So BoBo Muffkin and Maxi Muffkin went to see Tony Muffkin. There he was, munching on the hamburger BoBo Muffkin had brought him.

"Hey, kid, get me a glass of lemonade," Tony Muffkin demanded.

"I will be glad to get you lemonade as a friend," said BoBo Muffkin. "But not as a servant."

"Just get me the lemonade and stop fussing," Tony Muffkin demanded.

When Tony Muffkin said that, Maxi Muffkin looked angry. "Why didn't you say that to me?" he asked.

"You're my friend!" he said. "I wouldn't say that to a friend."

Suddenly Tony Muffkin knew what he had said. He looked at Maxi Muffkin. Maxi was his friend. He did not treat him like a servant. Then he looked at BoBo Muffkin. BoBo wanted to be his friend. So he knew that he should treat BoBo Muffkin the same way he treated Maxi Muffkin.

"I'm sorry, my FRIEND," Tony Muffkin said to BoBo Muffkin.

"That's all right, my FRIEND," said BoBo Muffkin.

Then Tony Muffkin went to get BoBo Muffkin a glass of lemonade so he could sit by the pool!

Aren't you glad Maxi Muffkin wrote all of this down so we could read it?

LET'S TALK ABOUT THIS
What this story teaches: Friends treat friends like friends, not like servants.
1. How do you treat your friends? How do they treat you? How should you treat each other?
2. How does Jesus want you and your friends to treat each other?

WHAT SHOULD I DO?

What Should I Do?

Numbers 22:1-20

"Look at those people!" said King Balak. "They will eat everything in our land!"

King Balak and his people were afraid. God had done many wonderful things for "those people," the Israelites. He had pulled apart the waters of a sea and let them walk through on dry land. He had fed them special food in the wilderness for years. He had given them His Law on Mount Sinai.

Balak and his people, the Moabites, had heard all of those things. They had heard that God had given the Promised Land to the Israelites.

Now they were afraid. The Israelites were on their way to the Promised Land. Would anything stop them?

Balak's neighbors, the Amorites, had not stopped them. When the Amorites attacked, the Israelites won and took their land. Balak's neighbors, the people of Bashan had not stopped them. When they attacked, the Israelites won and took their land. They even had a giant for a king. But that didn't help against the Israelites.

So Balak and his people were afraid. They were afraid to fight. And they were afraid not to fight.

"What should we do?" they asked.

Instead of asking God what to do, they tried to think of things on their own. Then someone had an idea.

"The Prophet Balaam!" someone shouted. "Give him lots of gold and silver. Tell him to curse the Israelites. If he curses them, they can't win!"

"But he is five hundred miles away!" said another. In those days five hundred miles seemed much farther. Even rich people had to walk or ride donkeys or camels.

"It's a great idea," said the king. "Bring him here!"

The king's officers bowed. They hurried away to find Balaam. What else could they do?

It took many days to reach Balaam's home. When they arrived, they told Balaam why they had come. Then they showed Balaam all the gold and silver they had brought.

"It's yours if you curse the Israelites," they said.

"What should I do?" Balaam wondered. Then he knew. He must ask God what to do.

"Wait here tonight," he told the king's officers. "I must ask God what to do. Tomorrow morning I will let you know."

Balaam must have looked sad the next morning. "I can't go," he told the king's officers. "God told me not to do it."

The officers went all the way back to Moab. They told the king what happened.

King Balak sent some other officers to see Balaam. They were more important than the others. They took more gold and silver than the others had taken.

"What should I do?" Balaam wondered when they offered him all that gold and silver. Then he knew. He must ask God what to do.

Nobody knows how Balaam prayed that night. But he probably didn't ask God. Instead, he must have told God why he should go and why God should let him go.

God was angry at Balaam. He would let Balaam go. But He did not want to.

"Go!" He told Balaam. "But don't do anything until I tell you!"

Balaam must have been awake much of that night. He wanted to go. God would let him go. But God didn't want him to go. "What should I do?" Balaam must have worried all night.

WHAT DO YOU THINK?
What this story teaches: What should we do when someone wants us to do wrong? Talk to God about it!
1. What did King Balak want Balaam to do? What did Balaam say? What did he do?
2. What Balak wanted was wrong. That's why God said no at first. Why do you think God said yes later?
3. What should you do when someone wants you to do wrong? Should you ASK God or try to tell Him why you should do it?

Toad for Lunch
A Muffin Family Story

"Hey, Maxi!"

"What, Pookie?"

"Guess what I saw behind the school?"

"What, Pookie?"

"A dead toad, that's what! And I want you to help me do something."

"What, Pookie?"

"We're going to put it in Charlie's lunchbox, OK?"

Maxi thought of Charlie. He could see Charlie opening his lunchbox and finding the dead toad. Then he could see Charlie not eating lunch. As soon as he saw that in his mind, Maxi saw the picture of Jesus on his wall. Maxi knew what Jesus would want!

"No, thanks, Pookie!" said Maxi. "Charlie wouldn't like that, and Jesus wouldn't like that."

"Chicken!" said Pookie. He walked away.

80

"Hey, Maxi!"

"What, BoBo?"

"Guess what I saw behind the school?"

"What, BoBo?"

"A dead toad, that's what! And I want you to help me do something."

"What, BoBo?"

"We're going to put it in Tony's lunchbox, OK?"

Maxi thought of Tony. He could see Tony opening his lunchbox and finding the dead toad. Then he could see Tony not eating lunch. As soon as he saw that in his mind, Maxi saw the picture of Jesus on his wall. Maxi knew what Jesus would want!

"No, thanks, BoBo!" said Maxi. "Tony wouldn't like that, and Jesus wouldn't like that."

"Chicken!" said BoBo. He walked away.

"Hey, Maxi!"

"What, Charlie?"

"Guess what I saw behind the school?"

"What, Charlie?"

"A dead toad, that's what! And I want you to help me do something."

"What, Charlie?"

"We're going to put it in Pookie's lunchbox, OK?"

Maxi thought of Pookie. He thought of how Pookie wanted to put the toad in Charlie's lunchbox. But he saw Pookie opening his lunchbox and finding the dead toad. Then he could see Pookie not eating lunch. As soon as he saw that in his mind, Maxi saw the picture of Jesus on his wall. Maxi knew what Jesus would want!

"No, thanks, Charlie!" said Maxi. "Pookie wouldn't like that, and Jesus wouldn't like that."

"Chicken!" said Charlie. He walked away.

"Hey, Maxi!"

"What, Tony?"

"Guess what I saw behind the school?"

"What, Tony?"

"A dead toad, that's what! And I want you to help me do something."

"What, Tony?"

"We're going to put it in BoBo's lunchbox, OK?"

Maxi thought of BoBo. He thought of how BoBo wanted to put the toad in Tony's lunchbox. But he saw BoBo opening his lunchbox and finding the dead toad. Then he saw BoBo not eating lunch. As soon as he saw that in his mind, Maxi saw the picture of Jesus on his wall. Maxi knew what Jesus would want!

"No, thanks, Tony!" said Maxi. "BoBo wouldn't like that, and Jesus wouldn't like that."

"Chicken!" said Tony. He walked away.

Maxi felt sad and alone. Would his friends want to be friends with him again?

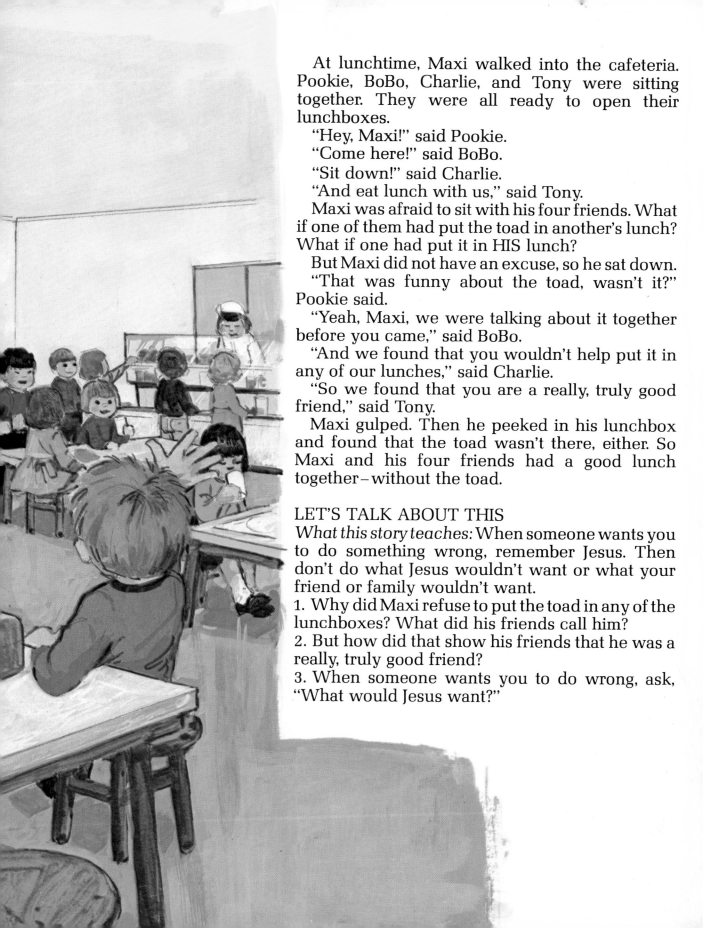

At lunchtime, Maxi walked into the cafeteria. Pookie, BoBo, Charlie, and Tony were sitting together. They were all ready to open their lunchboxes.

"Hey, Maxi!" said Pookie.

"Come here!" said BoBo.

"Sit down!" said Charlie.

"And eat lunch with us," said Tony.

Maxi was afraid to sit with his four friends. What if one of them had put the toad in another's lunch? What if one had put it in HIS lunch?

But Maxi did not have an excuse, so he sat down.

"That was funny about the toad, wasn't it?" Pookie said.

"Yeah, Maxi, we were talking about it together before you came," said BoBo.

"And we found that you wouldn't help put it in any of our lunches," said Charlie.

"So we found that you are a really, truly good friend," said Tony.

Maxi gulped. Then he peeked in his lunchbox and found that the toad wasn't there, either. So Maxi and his four friends had a good lunch together – without the toad.

LET'S TALK ABOUT THIS

What this story teaches: When someone wants you to do something wrong, remember Jesus. Then don't do what Jesus wouldn't want or what your friend or family wouldn't want.

1. Why did Maxi refuse to put the toad in any of the lunchboxes? What did his friends call him?

2. But how did that show his friends that he was a really, truly good friend?

3. When someone wants you to do wrong, ask, "What would Jesus want?"

Listen! Someone Is Talking!

Numbers 22:20-35

Balaam hurried around as if he were going to a party. He kept thinking of all the gold and silver the king offered him.

All he had to do was go back with the king's officers and curse the Israelites. Then the gold and silver would be his!

Balaam had asked God about this. But instead of asking, he must have argued. He probably told God ten good reasons for letting him do it.

"Go!" God had told him. But God was not happy about it. In fact, he was angry at Balaam.

God angrily watched Balaam get ready for the trip. He could go. But he would learn a lesson.

As Balaam traveled on his donkey, the Angel of the Lord suddenly stood in his way. The Angel had a sword in His hand, ready to kill him.

Balaam didn't see the Angel. But his donkey did! The donkey ran into a field.

Balaam was angry. What would those important people think? How could he curse a nation if he couldn't make his own donkey obey?

Balaam beat his donkey until it ran back into the road. But the Angel of the Lord stood in the way again.

This time the Angel of the Lord stood in a narrow path between two vineyards. There was a wall on each side of the road.

Balaam still did not see the Angel. His donkey did. It was afraid. But there was nowhere to run.

The donkey tried to squeeze past the Angel. When it did, it scraped along the wall and hurt Balaam's foot.

Balaam was more angry than before. He beat the donkey again.

Farther down the road the Angel stood once more with his sword drawn. This time the place was so narrow that the donkey could not even squeeze by. So it lay down in the road with Balaam on it.

Balaam was furious. He beat the donkey a third time.

Suddenly the Lord let Balaam's donkey talk. "Why did you beat me three times?" the donkey asked.

"Because you made me look foolish," Balaam answered. "If I had a sword, I would kill you."

"Have I ever done anything like this before?" the donkey asked.

"No," Balaam admitted.

Then the Lord let Balaam see the Angel standing there. He let him see the sword drawn, ready to strike him.

Balaam fell to the ground. "Why did you beat your donkey three times?" the Angel demanded. "I was ready to kill you. Your donkey kept me from doing it."

"I didn't know you were there," Balaam cried out. "I have sinned. I'll go home if you want me to."

"You may go on," the Angel said. "But say only what I tell you."

Balaam went on with the king's officers. But he had learned something very important. Do you know what?

WHAT DO YOU THINK?

What this story teaches: The Lord may let you do things that you want to do, even though He does NOT want you to do them. It's good to listen when someone else warns us that we are doing wrong.

1. Where was Balaam going? Did the Lord want him to go? Why did He let Balaam go?

2. What did the donkey see that Balaam didn't see? Why did the donkey do what it did?

3. Have you ever tried to talk the Lord into letting you do something? What should you do instead? ASK the Lord! LISTEN to others!

"Gopher Gulch" and a Sleepy Birthday

A Muffin Family Story

"But Mommi and Poppi! I'm a big girl now," Mini complained. "And ALL my friends are staying up late to watch "Gopher Gulch" on TV tonight."

"ALL of your friends?" asked Mommi.

Mini looked the other way. ALL meant some. Mini knew it, and Mommi and Poppi knew it.

"But it's only until midnight!" Mini argued.

"Mini, you know how tired you get when you stay up that late," said Poppi. "You will be so tired and grumpy tomorrow."

"But tomorrow's Saturday," said Mini. "And anyway it's my birthday."

"You don't want to be tired on your birthday, do you?" asked Mommi.

"I won't get tired," said Mini. "I'm a big girl now!"

Poppi looked at Mommi. Then he looked at Mini. "I think you should go to your room for a few minutes while Mommi and I talk about this," he said. "We'll call you when we have decided."

Mini ran to her room. Mommi and Poppi settled down in the living room to talk.

"This reminds me of the Bible story about Balaam that we read the other night," said Poppi. "Balaam wanted to do something. The Lord knew it was not right. But the Lord let him do it so Balaam would learn what was right."

"Are you saying we should let Mini do what she wants so she can learn it was not best for her?" Mommi asked.

"We can TELL Mini what we think is best," said Poppi. "But sometimes it's better for a boy or girl to LEARN what is best."

"I've heard the program is good, so we don't have to worry about that," said Mommi. "But I know Mini will be so tired for her surprise birthday party tomorrow night."

"But SHE is making that choice," said Poppi. "All of her life she'll have to choose between right and wrong, good and bad, better and best. This is a good time to think about those choices."

Mommi agreed. Mini would learn best by making her own choice this time.

When Mini came back, Poppi told her what he and Mommi had decided.

"This is the way it is," said Poppi. "Mommi and I think you should go to bed early tonight. We think you will enjoy your birthday more if you do not stay up late tonight."

"But I want to stay up," said Mini.

"If you want to do it, we will let you," said Poppi. "Even though we do not feel it is best for you. You must choose."

Mini was not as tired as she expected the next day. That is, not until late afternoon. Then she began to yawn. She even became a little grumpy.

She felt the most tired just before dinner when the doorbell rang. There were her friends, ready for the surprise birthday party.

"Surprise! Surprise!" they said. "We all went to bed early last night so we could stay up late tonight with you!"

Now Mini wished she had gone to bed early. None of her friends could talk about "Gopher Gulch." And it was hard to eat birthday cake when she was sleeping!

LET'S TALK ABOUT THIS
What this story teaches: We each must choose between good and bad, but we are wise to listen to others who may know more than we do.

1. Think of some times this past week when you had to choose between good and bad. What did you choose?

2. What choice did Mini have to make? How did she choose?

3. When you have to choose between good and bad, who can help you most? What can your parents do to help you? What can the Lord do to help you?

Say Something Good!

Numbers 22:36–24:25

"What took you so long?" King Balak asked Balaam.

The king had sent officers to Balaam. They had offered him much money if he would come with them and curse the Israelites. When Balaam refused, the king sent more officers and more money. This time Balaam came, even though the Lord did not want him to.

On the way the Angel of the Lord met Balaam. He was angry that Balaam was going. He almost killed Balaam.

"Say only what I tell you to say," He told Balaam.

Balaam went on his way to meet the king. But he was afraid. He certainly would say only what the Lord told him to say.

The king came to the border of his land to meet Balaam. He was anxious for Balaam to curse the Israelites. If he didn't, the Israelites might come into the king's land. They might take the king's land from him.

"What took you so long?" the king asked Balaam. "Didn't I tell you I would make you rich and important? Why did you wait so long to come?"

"I'm here now," said Balaam. "But I'll say only what the Lord tells me to say."

The king burned some animals on an altar. It was an offering to his gods. Then he gave Balaam some animals to keep.

The next morning the king took Balaam to a high mountain. Balaam and the king saw the Israelites camped in a valley below.

"Build seven altars," Balaam ordered. "Get seven young bulls and seven rams ready for the offering." The king told his people to do exactly what Balaam said. Then the animals were burned on the altars.

"Now wait here while I talk with the Lord," said Balaam. The king waited. Balaam climbed to a higher place to listen to the Lord.

King Balak was certainly surprised when Balaam came back. He did not curse the Israelites. Instead he said good things about them.

"What have you done to me?" the king demanded. He was angry. "I told you to curse these people. You have blessed them instead."

"But I told you I would say only what the Lord told me to say," Balaam answered.

The king took Balaam to a second mountain. "There!" said the king. "You can see only some of the Israelites. Curse them!"

Again the king offered animals on seven altars. Again Balaam asked the Lord what to say. But again he blessed them and did not curse them.

The king took Balaam to a third mountain. But Balaam blessed the Israelites again. This time he said even more wonderful things about them.

The king was furious. "Go home!" he shouted at Balaam.

Before he left, Balaam blessed the Israelites again. He said good things about them. But he also said things that weren't so good about the king's people.

Balaam went home. The king went home. And not one bad thing was said about the Israelites!

WHAT DO YOU THINK?
What this story teaches: Does someone want you to say bad things about others? Say good things instead.
1. What did the king want Balaam to say about the Israelites? What did Balaam say instead?
2. Has anyone wanted you to say bad things about others? What should you say instead? What will you do the next time someone wants you to say bad things?

My Good Friend

A Muffin Family Story

"Pookie's tooth makes him look like a squirrel, doesn't it, Maxi?" BoBo asked.

Maxi didn't want to say something bad about his friend Pookie. So he said something good instead.

"But have you ever noticed Pookie's eyes?" said Maxi. "I wouldn't be surprised if he is very handsome when he grows up."

BoBo looked surprised. "You really think so?" he asked. "Maybe you're right."

Bobo had just left when Pookie came along. "That Charlie is really stuck up, isn't he, Maxi?" Pookie asked.

Maxi didn't want to say something bad about his friend Charlie. So he said something good instead.

"But have you ever noticed how well Charlie does his schoolwork?" said Maxi. "I wouldn't be surprised if he becomes a brilliant man like Einstein when he grows up."

Pookie looked surprised. "You really think so?" he asked. "Maybe you're right."

Pookie had just left when Charlie came along. "That Tony is sure a cheapskate, isn't he, Maxi?" Charlie asked.

Maxi didn't want to say something bad about his friend Tony. So he said something good instead.

"But have you ever noticed how careful he is with his money?" said Maxi. "I wouldn't be surprised if he becomes a rich man like a Rockefeller when he grows up."

Charlie looked surprised. "You really think so?" he asked. "Maybe you're right."

Charlie had just left when Tony came along. "That BoBo is sure a bossy guy, isn't he, Maxi?" Tony asked.

Maxi didn't want to say something bad about his friend BoBo. So he said something good instead.

"But have you ever noticed what a good leader he is?" said Maxi. "I wouldn't be surprised if he becomes President or Prime Minister when he grows up."

Tony looked surprised. "You really think so?" he asked. "Maybe you're right."

A few minutes later BoBo saw Pookie. "Hey, Pookie," he said. "Have you ever noticed how you're getting so handsome?"

Pookie smiled a big smile. Then he ran over to a mirror to brush his hair.

A few minutes later Pookie saw Charlie. "Hey, Charlie," he said. "Do you know that you're going to be another Einstein some day?"

Charlie smiled a big smile. Then he tucked his books a little tighter under his arm and walked on.

A few minutes later Charlie saw Tony. "Hey, Tony," he said. "Do you know that you'll probably be a rich man some day?"

Tony smiled a big smile. He jingled the seventeen cents he had in his pocket and walked on.

A few minutes later Tony saw Bobo. "Hey, BoBo," he said. "Will you remember me when you're President or Prime Minister some day?"

Bobo smiled a big smile. He straightened his shirt collar and walked on.

A few minutes later BoBo saw Maxi. "Hey, Maxi," he said. "Do you know what a good friend you are to Pookie, Charlie, Tony, and me?"

Maxi smiled a big smile. Then he and his four friends went together to Pop's Sweet Shop for some ice cream.

LET'S TALK ABOUT THIS

What this story teaches: Saying good things is catching. Try it! Someone may even say something good about you!

1. What did Maxi do when each friend tried to say something bad about another friend? Did it work?
2. What happened when each friend said something good to another friend? How does this remind you of Balaam's saying good things about Israel?

Mini's Word List

Twelve words that all Minis and Maxis want to know:

ANGEL OF THE LORD–Angels are special beings who take care of God's people. God made them without bodies like ours. The Angel of the Lord seems to be the Lord Himself.

CHAINS–When people in Bible times were captured, they often had chains locked on their hands or feet. No one could take them off except the man with the key.

COURTYARD–Many houses have a wall around their yards. The space inside that wall is the courtyard. In Bible times a well or water tank was often in the courtyard.

DONKEY–In Bible times people often went from place to place by riding on a donkey. A donkey was also used to carry a heavy load.

FAITHFUL–A faithful person can be trusted completely. He or she will not turn against a friend.

GOD'S WORD–The Bible is sometimes called God's Word. It is also called the Scriptures. People in Jesus' time had only the Old Testament to read.

GREEK–Greek people were those who came from, or lived in, Greece. But in Jesus' time, the Jewish people sometimes spoke of all other people as "Greeks." It was another way of saying "Gentiles," or "people who are not Jews."

IDOLS–Idols were little statues made of wood or metal. They were shaped like people or animals or other objects. Some people thought idols were gods, or that a god worked through the idols.

LAMB OF GOD–Jesus was called the Lamb of God. In Bible times lambs were offered as sacrifices for sins. Jesus was offered for our sins on the cross.

LIONS' DEN–Daniel was thrown into a den of lions. It was a way to execute people. In Jesus' time, the Romans used a cross to execute people. Death on the cross was called "crucifixion."

MASTER–Slaves were common in Bible times. People who owned them were called "masters." Slaves were expected to obey their masters without argument. Christians serve the Lord, so we call Him Master.

WATER POTS–In Bible times people did not have water systems like ours. Water was often stored in big water pots, which were made of hard clay or of stone.